GRANNY
WITCH is the second in the
'Granny' series. The first was GRANNY
LEARNS TO FLY.

In this book Granny has decided to give up
flying but Spit still likes to take to the air
when no one is around. But one night he feels
he is being followed. Who can it be? An alien
from Outer Space?

TONY HICKEY, one of Ireland's best-
known writers for children and young people,
was born in Newbridge, County Kildare, and
spent most of this childhood there. Since then
he has lived in Dublin and London and
travelled extensively in Europe and America.

He has many TV, radio and screen credits
to his name and recently completed *Life
Dance,* a screenplay for Teddybear
Productions.

He is a member of the Writers in Schools
Scheme.

Tony Hickey

Granny and the American Witch

THE CHILDREN'S PRESS

First published 1998 by
The Children's Press
an imprint of Anvil Books
45 Palmerston Road, Dublin 6

2 4 6 5 3 1

ISBN 1 901737 13 6

*To my mother
and her grandchildren*

Typesetting by Computertype Limited
Printed by Colour Books Limited

Contents

1

Spit is Worried

Granny Green lived in a tiny house, which she called Tigín. The house stood at the entrance to the Valley of the Crows in County Wicklow

The valley got its name from the great flocks of crows that lived in the trees around the houses and cottages in the valley. These houses and cottages were now empty most of the time. The families that had lived in them had moved away, mainly to the town of Dara, where Granny's daughter and son-in-law, Mr and Mrs O'Brien, owned a hotel.

Granny Green loved the valley. She felt that she was in charge of it and that her house was like a sentry-post guarding the way in and out.

She was never lonely. She had plenty of friends, who came to see her. Her favourite visitors of all were her grandchildren, Sean and Maura, the O'Brien twins. Even when the weather was too bad for people to come to the Valley of the Crows, Granny Green had plenty of things to keep her happy. She had her books. She had her radio. She had her television. Most important of all, she had Spit, her beautiful black cat.

Spit was one of the cleverest cats that had ever lived. Not only could he talk to all the birds and animals in the valley; he could also speak to Granny and the twins and, thanks to him, they could also speak to the other creatures.

Even more extraordinary, Spit could fly. This he had learned from watching Granny Green teaching herself and her close friends to fly.

At first there had been a great deal of

excitement about the flying story. The valley had been crowded with news-paper and radio and TV reporters. Hundreds of ordinary people had been there too with their cars and vans and coaches, ruining the lovely fresh air of the valley with engine fumes and frightening away all the birds and animals with their noise.

When Granny made it quite clear that she was not going to teach anyone else, not even her own grandchildren, to fly, people lost interest in the story. Then the other flyers found that they could only fly when Granny Green was with them. No one knew why this should be.

'It must have something to do with the fact that Granny owns the book that the flying spell is in,' said Maura.

Sean nodded. 'You are probably right. Otherwise people everywhere could fly just by closing their eyes and taking three steps backwards and one step forward.'

'Maybe one day she will give us the book to keep. Then we will be able to fly like she does,' said Maura.

'Now then,' their mother said, 'you are not to go nagging your granny about this flying business. And anyway your father and I are not all that keen on the idea of the two of you flying around up there in the sky. Supposing there was an accident?'

'We'd be careful,' Maura said.

'Famous last words,' declared their father.

And that was the end of that.

Not that their parents needed to worry. Granny herself never mentioned flying except to say that she thought it best if she only flew in an emergency. 'Like when my little red car broke down. If that hadn't happened I would never have felt the need to fly at all. Now that the garage man has managed to fix it so cheaply for me, I can drive into Dara, as I have always done, to do my shopping.'

She also wanted to avoid doing anything that might bring the crowds back to the Valley of the Crows. She said, 'I think that it would be best to let things go back to normal.'

However Spit, the cat, had very different thoughts. He said, 'I think it's terrible not to fly if you know how. If you don't mind, Granny, I am going to go on flying.'

'Well don't attract the attention of strangers,' said Granny.

'Don't worry,' Spit said. 'I will be mucho careful. I will fly only when there is no one around. When I go into Dara to see Sean and Maura I will wait until after dark.'

The twins loved it when Spit came to visit them. He would tap gently at Maura's window until she woke up and let him in. Then he would slip quietly down the hall and wake Sean by tapping on his door.

The three of them would sit on the foot of Maura's bed and Spit would tell them all the news, not just about the Valley of the Crows, but also all the news from far away that he heard from other creatures that visited the valley.

One night, when Spit was, as usual, on Maura's bed, he suddenly stopped talking, jumped on the window-ledge and stared out into the night.

'What's wrong?' asked Sean.

Spit flicked his tail and said, 'It started a few days ago when I went to see the badger. He and I were having a very nice chat. Suddenly I had the feeling that someone was watching me. I looked all around but could see nothing.'

'And the badger noticed nothing?'

'No. And I didn't say anything to him in case I was imagining things,' replied Spit. 'But, on my way here tonight, I had the feeling that someone was following me.'

'Following you across the sky?' asked Maura. She and Sean sat on the ledge beside Spit and looked out at the star-filled sky.

'It's time I went back to Tigín,' the cat said.

'Spend the night here if you like,' said Maura. 'Sean and I could take you back to Tigín tomorrow on our bikes. Granny Green has invited us to lunch.'

'No, it's better if I fly home now. It will all probably turn out to be of no importance.'

Maura opened the bedroom window.

'We'll see you tomorrow. Safe home.'

The cat wagged his tail three times and flew away from the hotel. The twins watched until they could no longer see him. Suddenly the night sky looked very big and very lonely.

'Do you think that Spit is imagining things?' asked Maura. 'He always seems such a sensible cat.'

'I think he is more worried than he is saying,' said Sean. 'But who or what could follow him across the sky?'

'An alien,' suggested Maura.

'What would an alien want with Spit?' asked Sean.

'We might find out the answer to that tomorrow,' said Maura.

2

Where is Spit?

Next morning, as soon they had had breakfast and done their chores, the twins jumped up on their bikes and set off for the Valley of the Crows.

It was a beautiful sunny day with a light breeze that made it perfect cycling weather.

Granny Green was waiting for them at the gate of Tigín.

'We're not late, are we?' asked Maura as she and Sean leaned their bicycles against the garden wall.

'No, you are in plenty of time,' said Granny Green. 'I half expected Spit to be with you.'

'We haven't seen Spit since he left the hotel last night,' said Maura. 'Did he not come home?'

'I don't know. The cat-flap is always open for him to get in and out,' said Granny. 'I fell asleep in my armchair about ten o'clock and didn't wake up until after nine this morning.'

The twins said nothing. They were certain that Granny, without knowing it, was about to provide a clue as to what had happened to Spit.

Granny continued, 'It's the first time in my life that I slept all night in an armchair. I can't imagine what made me so tired. Spit may have got fed up waiting for me to wake up. He could have decided to go and watch them making that big war film down in Wexford. The crows were telling him all about it yesterday.'

'He'd hardly do that without letting you know,' said Maura. 'And he knew that we were coming to lunch.'

'He has always been a law unto himself, coming and going as he pleases,' said Granny, leading the way into the house. 'Don't forget that, unlike the humans, he can fly without me.'

She took a jug of lemonade out of the fridge and poured some for the twins. 'I dare say he will be back soon.' Then she saw the look that passed between Sean and Maura. 'Do the two of you know something that I don't?'

The twins remembered that Spit had said that he didn't want to worry Granny. They also remembered that the cat had been in the valley with the badger when he had first felt that he was being watched.

'Would you mind if we didn't answer your question now?' asked Sean. 'Maura and I will just nip up into the valley first to see if Spit is there.'

'This all sounds very serious,' said Granny Green.

'That's why we need to go and look for Spit before we say anything else,' explained Maura. 'We won't be long.'

Granny Green wasn't at all happy to let the twins go off by themselves without telling her why. She made them promise to be back in fifteen minutes; if they weren't, she would come looking for them.

As soon as they entered the valley Maura said, 'How quiet everything is. I know crows don't fly much in very hot weather but, even so, there are always some of them to be seen around the tops of the trees.'

By now they were at the tall rocks that looked down on the Durcans' empty farmhouse. Maura shaded her eyes against the sun. 'I thought I saw someone or something move down there near the old barn.'

'Let's investigate,' said Sean.

As they started towards the farm-house they both began to yawn. 'We can't be tired this early in the day,' groaned Sean.

Maura remembered what Granny had told them about falling asleep in her armchair and said, 'I have an idea. Let's go back to the rocks.'

As soon as they were back at the tall rocks the twins felt wide awake again. 'Now let's go back towards the farm-house,' said Maura.

At exactly the same spot as it had happened before, the twins began to yawn again.

Maura said, 'I think that there is something happening here that is making us sleepy. It made Granny sleepy last night. It could explain too why the crows are so quiet. It means that no one can go near the farmhouse and stay awake.'

Sean looked at his watch. 'We have less than ten minutes left before Granny comes looking for us. Let's go further into the valley. We might meet the badger or one of the other animals who can tell us what's going on.'

The twins walked quickly to where the badger usually was but, instead of him, they met a beautiful dog fox lying in the sun with his tail curled around his body. When he saw the children he tried to get up and run away. But after a few steps he yawned and fell down again.

'We won't hurt you,' said Maura.

The fox opened his sleep-filled eyes in surprise. 'I can understand what you are saying. Can you understand me?'

'Yes, we can,' said Sean. 'Why are you so sleepy?'

'I'm not sure,' yawned the fox. 'I arrived here for the first time last night. The place where I used to live was dug

up to make a new road. This place seemed nice and peaceful. I was on my way to have a look at the old barn down there when I just fell asleep.'

'How close to the old barn did you get?' asked Sean.

'Only as close as I am to it now,' said the fox. 'Then wham! total snooze time!'

'And you heard nothing and saw nothing strange?'

'No, not a thing,' said the fox.

'Move a bit closer to us,' said Maura.

The fox didn't seem very happy at this suggestion.

'It's all right. You will be safe and you will feel more awake,' said Sean.

The fox moved closer to the twins. 'You are right,' he said. 'I do feel more awake.'

'Move closer again.'

The fox's eyes brightened. 'Oh I see what you are getting at. The further I get away from the old farmhouse, the more wide awake I become. It's something down there that is making me fall asleep!'

'Yes,' said Maura. 'And now we need your help. You can slip through the bracken without being seen. Would you go to the farmhouse for us and see what's happening there?'

'You must be joking,' said the fox and ran away as fast as he could.

Meanwhile Granny Green was hurrying along the road towards them.

Sean looked at his watch again ... seven minutes to go before they were due back in Tigín. 'Maybe Spit came back,' he said to Maura.

'If he had, he'd be with Granny,' Maura said.

'I suddenly had second thoughts about our arrangement,' Granny Green announced as she reached the twins. 'I know that I said you could have fifteen minutes but a lot can happen in fifteen minutes and I am responsible for your safety while you are with me. Who was that fox that ran away from here?'

'We don't know his name but last night he suddenly fell into a deep, deep sleep just like you did,' said Sean. 'And we almost did, too, when we tried to go down to the old farmhouse.'

'And what has all this got to do with

Spit?' asked Granny. 'You might as well tell me everything.'

Granny Green listened carefully while the twins repeated what Spit had told them about the feeling he had of being watched while he was in the valley and being followed across the night sky.

Then she said, 'And you think that the answer to what has happened to Spit lies down there in the farmhouse?'

Maura said, 'We think that last night some kind of spell, maybe an alien spell, was put on the valley and on your house too. The spell affected every living creature. It made you all fall into a deep, deep sleep. Now the spell is lifting bit by bit. If we wait, we can go down to the farmhouse without falling asleep and see what's happening there.'

'I'm not sure that we ought to wait,' said Granny. 'Spit might be in serious trouble. I think we must get inside the farmhouse as quickly as possible before the aliens, if they are aliens, decide to take off. I think it is time for me to go flying again.'

'You'll have to let us fly with you,' said Sean. 'It might not be safe for you to go down there alone. This is a real emergency.'

'Very well,' said Granny. 'It is not as though you will be able to fly by yourselves so your parents can't complain. Now close your eyes. Three steps backwards. One step forward. And off we go.'

The twins felt the breeze suddenly become stronger. They opened their eyes. They were flying high above the valley. They caught sight of the dog fox. He was sitting in the heather, staring up at them in amazement.

Then they looked down and saw the tops of the trees around the old farmhouse. The nests there were full of

crows. Some of them were asleep.
Others were moving and shaking their
feathers.

'The sleeping spell must be almost
finished. The crows are starting to
wake,' said Granny. 'We have no time to
waste.'

3

Mystery at the Farmhouse

A pile of hay behind an old tractor made a safe and quiet place for Granny and the twins to land. Granny indicated to the twins that they should stay absolutely still until they knew if the sleeping spell was still working in the farmyard.

When none of them felt any need to yawn she made another sign; this time indicating that they should dash quickly across the yard to the open door of the barn. From there they had a clear view of the farmhouse.

At first glance everything looked much as it had been when Granny had given flying-lessons there.

Then they noticed a surfboard propped against the inside of one of the downstairs windows. Just as they were wondering what use a surfboard would be in the Valley of the Crows, they smelled turf burning. A trickle of smoke came from one of the chimneys.

'Aliens wouldn't light a fire. Someone must be living here. How could they have moved in without me seeing them go past Tigín?' Granny whispered. 'And what kind of person would be able to put us all under a sleeping spell? The two of you had better wait here while I go on a fly-around. If anything bad happens to me go and fetch your parents from Dara.'

Granny flew up into the air. She looked in through the first bedroom window. She could just about make out a sleeping-bag and two open suitcases, filled with clothes, on the floor.

She moved to the next window and saw the landing at the top of the stairs. Through a third window she saw a very old-fashioned bathroom. There were three more upstairs windows belonging to three totally empty bedrooms. So it would seem that there was only one person in the house. Judging from the clothes in the suitcases that person was a woman.

The twins hardly dared to breathe as Granny Green turned her attention to the downstairs windows of the house. The first two rooms seemed to have nothing of interest in them. Then she looked into the room with the surfboard. At once her expression changed to one of excitement. She turned and moved her hand through the air.

'That's Spit that she is drawing in the air,' Sean exclaimed, forgetting that he was supposed to be quiet. 'Granny has found Spit!'

The sound of his voice roused the still-sleepy crows from their nests and sent them screaming and wheeling into the sky like a huge dark cloud.

Almost at once the door of the farmhouse opened. A tall, thin woman, wearing a flowery dressing-gown, came out and looked up at the birds.

'Darn and tarnation,' she said in an American accent. 'The sleeping spell has worn off sooner than I thought it would.'

Then she saw Granny Green hovering

several feet above the ground. 'Who are you? And what are you doing here?'

'I have come to collect my cat Spit,' Granny replied.

'Your cat? Well I have news for you. The cat in this house belongs to ME.'

'Oh no, he does not. He belongs to ME. Or maybe I should say that he lives with me in my little house, which he would never willingly leave. You have kidnapped him,' declared Granny.

'Are you sure you don't mean "cat-napped"?' sneered the woman in the dressing-gown.

Maura and Sean decided it was time for them to interrupt before the women got really angry with each other. They stepped out of the barn.

'Why don't you ask Spit where he belongs?' asked Maura.

'That's right. That's right,' crowed the crows, who had stopped cawing and were listening to what was happening in the farmyard. 'Spit can talk for himself. He is his own boss, always has been, always will be!'

'Now that's a very good idea,' said Granny. 'Let's ask him right now where he belongs.'

'No one goes into my house without my permission. And certainly not a witch.' The woman placed herself firmly in the middle of the doorway.

Maura said, 'Our granny is not a witch.'

'Then how come she can fly? I'll bet she has an invisible broomstick.'

'I most certainly do not have an invisible broomstick,' said Granny. 'And this is not your house. It belongs to the Durcans.'

'Not any more, it doesn't. I bought it from them two weeks ago. They are using the money to buy a huge apartment in Newbridge.'

Granny Green got such a surprise when she heard this that she forgot to continue hovering and fell in a heap on the ground. The twins rushed forward to help her to her feet.

'That was all your fault,' Sean said to the woman in the dressing-gown.

'It most certainly was not my fault,' said the woman. 'It was the fault of all of you coming around here where you have no right to be. Now go away. One witch per valley is quite enough.'

'One witch per valley? Does that mean that you are a witch then?' asked Sean. 'Is that how you were able to move in here without Granny seeing you? Is that how you were able to follow Spit across the sky? We thought he might have been followed by an alien.'

'Well now you know that you were wrong. Get off my property!'

Granny smoothed down her frock. 'We will not go away from here until we talk to Spit.'

'He doesn't want to talk to you,' the witch snapped back.

'That's because he is still under the sleeping spell. It has lifted from Tigín and the valley but it is still working inside the farmhouse. If Spit wasn't under the sleeping spell, the sound of my voice would have brought him out to see what was going on,' Granny said. 'If we can't go into the house to talk to him, then we will just wait here until he wakes up.'

'And what's to stop me from making another sleeping spell that will put you all asleep forever?' asked the woman.

'I was wondering the same thing,' said Maura. 'Just now you were complaining because the sleeping spell wore off too soon. Maybe all your spells wear off too soon. Maybe you aren't a very good witch. Is that why you stole Spit? Is it because a witch is supposed to have a black cat and Spit is the cleverest black cat of all? Did you steal him because he might help you become a better witch?'

The witch went red with rage. 'I did not steal Spit. He belongs to me. And as for not being very good at casting spells, let's see what you think of this.'

She snapped her fingers. The farmhouse and the trees around it vanished. For a few seconds, Granny and the twins and the crows stared open-mouthed and open-beaked at the empty space where the farmhouse and the trees had been.

Then the crows began to crash into each other and to shriek, 'Our homes! Our nests! Gone! Gone! All gone and it's all your fault for upsetting the witch!' They swooped down over Granny and the twins, who angrily waved them away.

'You are being stupid,' Sean said to them. 'Spit is your friend. You should be doing something to help us to get him back.'

'Such as what?' the crows demanded.

'We don't know yet but we will think of something. Won't we, Granny?' said Maura.

Granny said, 'Maybe we should go back to Tigín and read through my book of spells. There might be something there to help us!'

4

The Fox Comes Back

As Granny and the twins flew back to Tigín, Granny said, 'Well at least we now know who it was that followed Spit across the sky. It was that witch. She used the sleeping spell to capture him.'

'She doesn't think of it as "capturing",' said Sean. 'She seems to truly believe that he belongs to her!'

'How on earth could she believe that?' Granny sounded cross. 'Spit has lived with me since I found him as a tiny kitten on the side of the road.'

'Have you never wondered how he came to be on the side of the road?' asked Maura.

'Oh don't tell me you are on the side of the witch,' said Granny.

'No, of course not,' said Maura. 'But it

is interesting that she should think that you are a witch.'

'And what exactly does that mean?' demanded Granny.

'Well, there was that book of spells that you found in the attic.'

'Are you suggesting that I might be a witch and not know it?'

'I was really thinking about your great-grandmother who wrote down the spells,' said Maura. 'She could have been a witch.'

'All this will have to wait until we rescue Spit,' said Granny.

She went into the sitting-room where she kept the book of spells in a locked box under the sofa. Because the book was so old she had to turn the pages very carefully.

The twins watched anxiously as she read each page, hoping that there was something there about making houses visible again but there was nothing that could help them.

An animal barked outside. 'That sounds like the fox,' said Sean.

Sean was right. The fox was standing at the front gate. 'Hey, there,' he said. 'Pardon me for asking but what exactly is going on?'

'I thought you didn't want to get mixed up in any of it,' said Maura.

'I didn't at first,' said the fox. 'After all I came to the valley to get away from trouble. But when I saw the three of you flying through the air, I thought that maybe I should hang about and ask some questions. I may be able to help.'

'Can you make an invisible house visible?' asked Granny. 'Spit, the cat, is inside it, at the mercy of that witch.'

'Why don't you just go inside the house and rescue Spit?' asked the fox. 'Just because you can't *see* the house doesn't mean that you can't touch it and find the door.'

'And what if the witch attacks us?' asked Granny.

'I don't think she is all that good a witch,' said the fox.

'Maura said that too,' said Granny. 'Yet the witch made the house and the trees disappear.'

'I think she was as surprised as anyone that that spell worked,' said the fox. 'As I was passing the big rocks just now I saw her walking around the farmyard. It looked to me as though she was checking that the house and the trees had actually disappeared. Maybe her problem is that she never knows for sure when a spell is going to work.'

'And that could mean that she doesn't know when the spell is going to stop working,' said Sean. 'The farmhouse could become visible any moment.'

'Even if it doesn't, we can still find it by touching it, just like the fox has said,' declared Maura.

'We must go back to the farmhouse at once,' said Granny. 'Thank you very much, Mr Fox.'

'My friends used to call me "Chicken" because chickens were once my favourite food,' said the fox. 'Now I'm thinking of becoming a vegetarian. That way I am hoping that humans will let me alone.'

'If you really want to be safe you should change your name as well as your eating habits,' said Maura. 'Why don't you call yourself "Veggie"?'

'Veggie the fox? I like the sound of that,' said the fox. 'From now on I am Veggie the fox. Now, last back to the farmhouse is a hedgehog!'

Veggie ran into the Valley of the Crows. Granny and the twins took to the air but the fox was so fast and so good at taking short cuts that he reached the farmhouse well ahead of them.

The crows were still making a terrible row. It became even louder when they saw Veggie. 'Get away from here,' they yelled. 'No foxes allowed!'

Then they saw Granny and the twins and flocked around them.

'Oh do be quiet,' Granny said. 'How is a person supposed to think, much less fly safely, with all of you crowding around like this? Go back to the trees.'

'Trees? What trees? You need to put your flying goggles on, Granny! The trees are all gone!'

'Just because you can't see them doesn't mean that they aren't still there,' said Sean. 'Veggie, the fox, told us that.'

'That's right,' barked Veggie. 'And you don't have to worry about me. I would die rather than eat crow.'

The crows ignored this remark and

flew back to where the tops of the trees should have been. 'You are right. We can feel the branches under our feet.' They settled down on the invisible branches.

'Now for the farmhouse,' said Granny. She and the twins landed in the farm-yard and walked with their hands out in front of them to where the farmhouse should have been.

'I can feel the wall. And here's a window,' Granny said. 'The back door must be very close to where the two of you are standing.'

The twins felt their way along the wall and suddenly touched the door. 'You are right. The back door is here.'

'Can you open it?' Veggie asked

Maura tried the latch. 'Yes.'

It was the strangest feeling in the world for the twins to push open the invisible back door and walk into the visible kitchen on the other side.

The witch was sitting at the table, looking through a book of spells. 'Drat! I should have known that you two would come back to annoy me. But at least you seem to have left Grandma at home this time.'

'Oh no, they haven't,' Granny Green said but, before she could step into the kitchen, the witch clicked her fingers. The back door slammed shut and locked itself.

For a second the witch looked amazed that the spell had worked. Then she said, 'I'd like to see your grandmother get that door open in a hurry!'

'And we'd like to see you unlock it by clicking your fingers again,' said Sean. 'You didn't know whether or not the spell was going to work until it did. If you are all that clever you'd have locked all the doors when you made the house invisible.'

'Well you two might not be as clever as you think either,' snapped the witch. 'Now that you are in my house I have you in my power. No one can get in to help you.'

Granny Green banged on the back door. 'Open this door at once. If you touch a hair on my grandchildren's heads you will be sorry for the rest of your life!'

'Don't worry, Granny, we are all right.

She can't keep the house invisible forever. All her spells wear off sooner than she expects,' Maura called out. 'We are going to get Spit.'

'You will do no such thing.' The witch pointed at the door into the hall and clicked her fingers. But the door stayed open. 'Drat and tarnation!'

'We were right. You don't really know when a spell is going to work,' laughed Sean.

The twins rushed into the room where the surfboard was. 'Spit, it's us! Maura and Sean! We've come to rescue you!'

The room was empty.

'She has moved him. He must be upstairs.'

They started up the stairs but before they reached the landing the house gave a lurch that knocked them back down into the hall. There was the sound of furniture falling over in the kitchen, followed by a loud scream from the witch. The twins scrambled to their feet.

'The witch sounds as though she is in trouble,' gasped Sean.

That was all he had time to say before the house lurched in the opposite direction. The twins were thrown up on to the landing. More furniture fell over downstairs. The witch screamed again. A seagull crashed into the window, looked startled, and flew off complaining. A wisp of cloud came into view and vanished.

'I think we're up in the sky,' Maura shouted.

A bedroom door opened. Spit came strolling out, yawning slightly. 'What's going on?' he asked, as calmly as if he was at home in Tigín.

'We seem to have taken off,' answered Sean. 'The witch in the kitchen has made the farmhouse fly. The question is: Did she mean that to happen – and has she any idea what to do next?'

'I'll bet she was trying to figure out how to make the house stay invisible and got the spells mixed up,' said Maura.

'I think you are right,' said Spit. 'She made a terrible mess of capturing me last night. The first spell that she tried made it snow. The second one turned everything, including me, bright yellow. The third one turned her surfboard into a biscuit tin. We almost fell off it as we were taking off.'

'So that's what she uses the surfboard for,' said Sean. 'To fly through the sky.'

'Yes, it seems that broomsticks are very old-fashioned, although some witches still use them for short trips. But for long journeys a surfboard is better. She says that she flew all the way across the Atlantic ocean on it.'

'But why didn't you try to escape? Couldn't you have jumped off the board and flown home?' asked Maura.

'She said that she would do something terrible to Granny Green if I tried to get away,' said Spit. 'And the closer the surfboard got to the farmhouse the more sleepy I began to feel. In fact I was fast asleep before we touched down. I think the witch was affected by the spell too. My last memory of last night is of her yawning and yawning. I suppose I should consider myself lucky that she managed to get us both safely inside the house. She could easily have fallen asleep and crashed the surfboard into the barn.'

'Let's hope that she isn't as bad a witch as we think she is. We don't want her to crash this house into anything,' said Sean.

5

The Flying House

As Granny tried once more to force open the locked, invisible back door, she felt what seemed like a sudden rush of warm air on her face and a great whoosh! of something moving through the air. She stepped back in surprise as the grass around her feet bent over and the tin roof of the old barn rattled.

'What was that?' she asked the fox.

Veggie pointed to a great flat space, which marked the place where the farmhouse had stood. 'I think the witch has managed to make the house fly.'

'Now what am I going to do?' asked Granny.

'Go after the house, of course,' said Veggie. 'You're forgetting what I told you back at Tigín. Just because something is invisible doesn't mean that it isn't there. And that means, while the house is crossing the sky, it will still cast a shadow on the ground.'

'But the sky is so big and I don't know where the witch has taken the house,' said Granny.

'Make the crows help you.'

The crows, who had been listening to this conversation, shook their heads and said, 'Oh no. Leave us out of it. You can be a do-gooder but not us.'

'I am not a do-gooder. I am thinking only of myself,' said Veggie. 'Just like you, I want to live in this valley with no trouble from humans. Think of what will happen if the story of the witch gets out. Everyone for miles around will come here. The valley will probably end up being called the Valley of the Witch.'

'Oh we don't want that. We don't want that,' cried the crows. 'We will help in any way that we can. Granny, what do you want us to do?'

'I think that you should split into four groups and fly in four different directions – north, south, east and west. When you find the house, sit on the roof and call out as loudly as you can. I will fly around as well, in case I should find the house by myself.'

'What's the fox going to do?' asked the senior crow.

'I'm going to follow along on the ground,' said Veggie. 'Now, move before the house ends up so far away that we will never reach it.'

The crows took off first, dividing into four groups as Granny Green had suggested. She went next, zooming straight up into the sky. When she looked down, the fox was just a bright orange dot running along the valley.

Then she noticed a strange shadow

moving across the countryside and remembered the words of the fox: 'While the house is crossing the sky, it will cast a shadow on the ground.'

Granny flew above the shadow. At once she felt cooler. It was as if she were sitting under a large tree. That meant that the invisible house was above her and shading her from the sun. She flew higher, keeping her hands stretched above her head.

Within seconds she touched the corner of the house. She felt carefully along the side until she touched what felt like a door – which might still be locked. She didn't want to let the witch know that she had caught up with the house by forcing her way in through the door. An upstairs window would be the best way to get into the house without attracting attention.

Granny moved up along the outside

of the invisible house until she felt glass beneath her fingers. She had reached one of the bedroom windows! She found the upper half of the window and pulled. To her great relief it wasn't locked and opened easily and quietly. She stuck her head in and, like the twins, found it very strange to be able to see inside a house the exterior of which was invisible.

The north-flying crows found it even more weird for, when they turned around to see where Granny was, all they could see was that part of her body that was still outside the window. It looked to them as though someone had cut off Granny's head.

'Murder!' they began to scream. 'Murder! Someone has cut off Granny Green's head!'

The other three groups of crows heard the shouting and looked back. They all began to shout. 'Granny Green has had her head cut off! The witch must have done it! The witch must have done it!'

'Oh dear,' Granny said to herself. 'If people on the ground look up and see what looks like a headless woman in the sky, they will call the guards and the newspapers. I must get into the house immediately before the witch hears what the crows are saying.'

But the witch had already heard the crows. So too had Spit and the twins.

Spit burst into tears. 'Granny Green without a head? It's all my fault.'

Then there was a thump in the room overhead. The crows yelled, 'Granny Green has vanished! Granny Green has vanished!'

Spit stopped crying and grinned at the twins. 'If that thump wasn't Granny arriving upstairs, then I'm a cheese-eating mouse.'

The twins followed him up to the unused bedroom. There, somewhat out of breath and brushing dust off her frock, was Granny Green.

'Thank goodness you are all right,' said Maura.

'Yes, I'm fine,' Granny smiled.

'Why did the crows think that you had lost your head?' asked Sean.

'Because they couldn't see it when I looked in through the window,' said Granny. 'Then, when I managed to climb in through the window, they thought that the rest of me had vanished. I am surprised that the witch hasn't come rushing up to see what's going on.'

'She's trapped behind the furniture in the kitchen,' Spit said. 'Every time the house lurches the furniture moves. So she can't get out from behind it.'

'She's not hurt, is she?' asked Granny.

'No, just very, very cross,' said Spit.

'I think we'd better go down and have a word with her,' said Granny. 'We can't go on rushing across the sky in an invisible farmhouse. Something terrible might happen.'

The witch was far from pleased when Granny led the others into the kitchen. She scowled and shook her fist but that was all she could do, for the heavy kitchen table kept her pressed against the wall. Upturned chairs and a dresser,

with all its crockery smashed, lay on the floor.

'Well this is a nice mess and no doubt,' Granny said as she stepped carefully over things.

'Nobody asked you to get mixed up in it,' said the witch

'Oh, and what did you think I was going to do?' asked Granny. 'Just sit around in Tigín while you made off with my grandchildren and Spit?'

The house gave another lurch. The dresser moved across the floor and the chairs banged into each other. The kitchen table slid away from the witch and towards the window.

'Now's your chance to get free!' Granny said, grabbing the witch and pushing her out into the sitting-room. Spit and the twins followed and got out of the kitchen just before the dresser moved yet again and jammed the kitchen door from the inside.

'Aren't you even going to thank Granny Green for rescuing you?' Maura asked.

The witch tossed her head. 'I could have got out of there by myself if I had wanted to.'

'But, of course, you didn't want to,' Spit said scornfully. 'You liked being trapped behind that table, just as you like flying across the sky in a house that you don't know how to steer.'

'I could steer it if I wanted to,' muttered the witch.

'Then the sooner you start, the better,' said Granny. 'We are getting very close to the highest mountains in Wicklow.'

The twins looked out of the window and gasped in horror as the house skimmed the top of a mountain.

A group of climbers, enjoying a picnic there, were almost blown over as the house passed directly above their heads. They had barely recovered from this shock when the crows came calling and yelling across the sky.

'Those people must think it was a flying saucer passing overhead,' said Maura. 'They are rushing down off the mountain. They must be going to call the guards.'

'No one will take them seriously,' said the witch.

'The Air Corps will if we show up on their radar screens,' said Sean. 'In fact I think that I can hear the sound of planes right now.'

Sean was right. Two planes, shining like silver in the bright sunlight, suddenly appeared on the horizon.

'They could crash into us!' Granny looked at the witch as though she was going to give her a good shaking. 'You have to do something immediately.'

'She can't do anything,' said Spit. 'She's a terrible witch. She doesn't really know how to make spells work.'

'And, anyway, her book of spells is in the kitchen and we can't get in there now,' said Sean.

'Is there not a phrase that undoes all spells?' asked Maura.

'Yes, there is,' said the witch. 'But I don't see why I should use it to help any of you.'

'It is not just us you'll be helping, you'll be helping yourself as well,' said Granny.

The planes were now so close to the house that the pilots' puzzled faces could be seen. And the speed at which they were travelling was causing vibrations that made the old farmhouse groan.

'The house will fall to bits if you don't say the phrase that undoes spells but, please, try to get it right,' Spit said to the witch. 'And remember that we don't want the house to become visible while those planes are looking for us. We just want to land safely on the ground when there's no one watching.'

The stairs banister began to wriggle like a snake. Suddenly it popped out of position and swung around the hall.

Sean said, 'Spit is right. The house is breaking up.'

Maura looked out of the window and screamed, 'There's a huge pine forest straight ahead!'

Every nail and bolt and board in the house was trembling and shaking now. Soon it wouldn't matter if the witch said the words which would stop the house flying. The house would break apart, scattering everyone and everything in it to the four winds.

Then the planes zoomed up and away from the house.

'What's happening?' asked Granny.

'They were too close to the tree-tops for safety,' said Sean. 'But just look at the way the trees are bending.'

The speed at which the planes had flown back up into the sky had created a wind storm that made the entire pine forest bend and wave.

The crows got caught up in this new gale and were blown around the sky like pieces of burnt paper.

'Say the words now before the planes come back!' Spit had to shout at the witch to make himself heard above the noise of the wind. 'UNDO THE FLYING HOUSE SPELL!'

Suddenly the house slowed down. Then it floated gently down to the ground and landed safely in a clearing where trees had recently been cut down.

The humans all stared at Spit.

'You clever cat,' said Granny. 'You've

saved us and the house.'

'It was all by chance,' said Spit. 'I was really asking the witch to lift the spell when I shouted: "UNDO THE FLYING HOUSE SPELL."'

'Nonsense,' said the witch. 'What you did proves that you belong to me. You knew all along how to stop the house from flying.'

'But that means that you must have known as well,' said Sean. 'Even a baby could remember how to stop a spell from working if all you have to say is, "Undo the spell."'

'We can talk about this much more seriously later on,' said Granny. 'The planes might come back at any second.'

6

Danger in the Pine Forest

Meanwhile the crows had seen the cloud of dust that had risen from the ground when the invisible house had landed. Now they were screeching and swooping around and sitting on the invisible roof.

'If the pilots see dozens of crows sitting on nothing they will send some of the forest workers up here to investigate,' Granny said. 'We need to get the crows back to the valley as soon as possible!'

'Why don't you just tell them to go back there by themselves?' asked the witch.

'That makes sense,' said Spit. 'And, if they all formed into one big group the pilots might think that that was what they saw on their radar screens. That sort of things happens all the time. When people think that they are seeing flying saucers, it usually turns out to be a plane or a cloud.'

'Usually but not always,' the witch said.

'You believe in aliens and all that stuff?' asked Spit.

'Oh yes, I do. I could tell you stories that would raise the fur on the back of your neck,' said the witch.

'The planes are coming back,' cried Maura.

'Leave it all to me. I'll go and talk to the crows,' said Spit. 'If the pilots see me they will think that I am a cat out hunting. But first I have to unlock the door.'

He pointed his tail at the door and said: 'UNLOCK THE DOOR!' The door swung open. Spit grinned happily. 'Hey, this is a very useful trick.'

'It is *not* a trick. It's a magic power,' said the witch but Spit just grinned again in reply before stepping out into the sunlit clearing.

'Now then, birdies,' he said to the crows. 'We thank you very mucho for your help. If you want to go on helping us, the best thing would be if you all got together and winged it back to the valley. The planes are bound to follow you. When you arrive there, just behave as though nothing strange has happened. You will probably find that the invisible spell has worn off and that you will be able to see the trees again.'

'Why hasn't it worn off the house then?' It was Veggie, the fox, stepping daintily through the undergrowth.

'I think it's because the witch got two spells mixed up,' said Spit. 'Who are you anyway?'

'I'm Veggie, the fox. I arrived in the valley just as all the excitement began. Which two spells did she get mixed up?'

'I think that, instead of making the house fly, she wanted to put the sleeping spell on the valley again.'

'What good would that have done? She couldn't keep everyone asleep forever.'

'Maybe she wanted time to decide what to do next about Granny Green and me. As you may have guessed, she is not a very clever witch.'

Then Spit noticed that the crows were still there, listening. 'Have you lot not gone yet?'

'We don't want to miss anything,' said the senior crow. 'After all we were in at the very beginning of this story. It is only fair that we should know what's going to happen next.'

'I promise to tell you every detail

when we meet in the Valley of the Crows,' said Spit. 'Now please go or we will all be in serious trouble.'

The two planes came roaring back in across the mountains and swooped down over the forest.

The crows rose up like a great blanket of feathers, almost blocking out the sun. The planes flew around and around in a circle as though deciding what to do.

'We need to find out where the pilots are going to go next,' Spit said to Veggie. 'You wait here.'

The cat flew up under the flock of crows and landed unseen on the top of the first plane. He could just about hear Pilot One speaking to Pilot Two.

'Pilot One to Pilot Two: Do you see what I see, Harry?'

'Pilot Two to Pilot One: Yes, Charlie. I see a flock of crows. Could this be what we saw on our radar?'

'Pilot One to Pilot Two: Yes, Harry, it could be. I am going to report back to base.'

The officer in charge of the air base was furious when he heard what Pilot One had to say. He snapped, 'A flock of crows? You've been out chasing a flock of crows?'

Just then the telephone next to him rang. He answered it, still feeling very cross.

'Hello.' He listened. Then his face brightened and he said, 'Hold on.'

He spoke to Pilot One again: 'Pilot One. Air Base to Pilot One.'

'Pilot One to Air Base: I can hear you loud and clear.'

'A group of mountain climbers has just reported what sounds like a craft from outer space passing over their heads close to where you are. Keep an eye out for invisible flying objects.'

'Pilot One to Base. Pilot One to Base: How can I keep an eye out for invisible objects? How can I see an invisible object?'

Pilot Two interrupted. 'Pilot Two to Pilot One. Pilot Two to Pilot One: There is something strange going on down there in that clearing that the crows just flew up from. I can see smoke but no fire.'

The officer in charge shouted, 'What does that mean?'

'It means that I can see smoke rising in the air. Out of nowhere.'

Spit realised that the smoke the pilot was seeing was from the chimney of the invisible farmhouse.

'I can see it too!' Pilot One said. 'It could be coming from an invisible space-craft. That flock of crows could be aliens in disguise. They could be off to attack some town or city.'

The officer at the base said, 'Pilot One, you hang around there and keep an eye on the clearing. We will send helicopters and forestry workers to check out the smoke. Pilot Two, you follow the crows and see what they get up to. Over and out.'

As Pilot Two set off after the crows, Pilot One tilted his plane so that he could return to the mountains and come back in more slowly over the forest.

The tilt caught Spit by surprise. He slid down the top of the plane and landed on the nose of the plane. Pilot One gasped in amazement as he and the cat looked at each other through the window of the cockpit. Then Spit jumped off the plane and flew down to the clearing.

Pilot One was about to call the base again. Then he thought, 'I must be imagining things. Aliens disguised as crows! Smoke without fire! Now a black cat looking in at me through the window! Who would ever believe me? Unless of course it's all part of a plot by the aliens to drive us crazy?

'I will just do as I'm told. Yes, yes, I will just do as I'm told. Which means that all I have to do is to keep an eye on the clearing until the helicopters and the forestry workers arrive.'

He whizzed off across the sky as Spit

landed beside Veggie and said, 'One plane has gone after the crows but the pilot in the other plane saw me. And both of them saw the smoke from the kitchen chimney. They are sending helicopters and forestry workers to investigate. We'd better get inside the house and warn the others.'

They found the door and rushed into the kitchen.

'Throw water on the fire,' Spit cried. 'The pilots can see the smoke!'

They all pushed at the kitchen door until they managed to open it.

Sean poured water from the kettle on to the fire. Smoke began to fill the kitchen, making everyone cough.

'We can't stay here. We will suffocate,' Granny said to the witch. 'There must be a spell that can help us. Look in your book.'

'I know what spells are in the book.

There is nothing about a smoke-filled kitchen,' the witch snapped. 'The best thing we can do is to open the windows and hope that the smoke will vanish before the plane comes back.'

'I think it's the helicopters and the forestry workers that we need to worry about now,' said Veggie. 'The helicopters could easily land in this clearing. We need to get the house out of here – and it's no longer safe for us to fly across the sky.'

'If we can't fly, how can we move the house?' asked the witch.

'What about making things smaller?' asked Granny. 'Can you make this house and everything in it smaller, without making it visible?'

'Yes, I suppose so.'

'Well, if you can make that happen, Sean and Maura can go outside and carry us and the house back to the

Valley of the Crows,' said Granny.

Veggie nodded in agreement with this suggestion. 'I'll go outside with the twins. I can show them secret short cuts through the forest and across the mountains to the valley.'

As the twins and Veggie left the house they heard the sound of the plane on its way back. They could also hear the buzz of helicopters approaching from another direction. They slammed the door of the house shut and ran to hide in among the trees until the danger had passed.

7

Pigs Can Fly

Meanwhile back in the cottage the witch thumbed through her book of spells. 'This one might do,' she mumbled.

'Read it out, just to be sure,' said Spit.

The witch read the words of the spell: LET THIS HOUSE, THAT'S FAR TOO BIG, BE SMALL ENOUGH TO HOUSE A PIG!

There was a sound like air coming out of a balloon. 'It's getting smaller all right – and so are we,' said Granny. 'But it's still too big for the twins to carry.'

'To carry where exactly?' asked a new voice. A bright pink pig came in from the hall.

'How did you get into my house?' demanded the witch.

'Your house?' asked the pig. 'This is my house. Just now I wished for a place of my own and the pig-fairy has granted my wish by sending me to this place.'

'But this is a house for humans,' the witch said.

'Well it is certainly untidy enough for humans, with all that broken furniture around the place, but I can soon tidy up all that,' said the pig.

'There has been a mistake,' said Granny. 'How would you like to be able to fly across the sky until you find the real home of your dreams?'

'Sounds terrific!' the pig said.

'Then just do as I do,' said Granny.

The pig watched while Granny flew around the room several times. Then he said, 'I think I know how to do it now!'

He made two perfect flights around the kitchen and then flew through the window. Granny said, 'Happy house hunting,' and closed the window.

The plane came back overhead just as

the pig appeared as if from nowhere.

Pilot One at once called the air base and the men in the helicopters.

'I have just seen a flying pig heading for the city. This pig could be another alien in disguise.'

The officer at the air base shouted, 'Everyone is to follow that flying pig. Don't let it out of your sight whatever you do. The forestry workers can take care of the stuff on the ground.'

The plane and the helicopters all set off across the sky after the pig, watched by the fox and the twins, who were every bit as surprised to see the flying pig as the pilots were.

'I didn't know there was a pig in the house.' Veggie sounded puzzled.

'The witch has got things wrong again,' chuckled Maura.

'Maybe so,' said Veggie, 'but she has also managed to get rid of that plane and those helicopters. I wonder how big the house is now. Pity we can't see it. We'd know if we'd be able to carry it.'

Spit stepped out into the clearing. 'Maybe I can make it visible, just like I stopped it from flying.'

He cleared his throat and said in a very deep voice, 'UNDO THE INVISIBLE HOUSE SPELL.'

The house, now a quarter of its original size, appeared in the clearing.

'That is very impressive,' said Veggie.

'But it is still far too big for us to carry,' said Sean. 'Try making it smaller.'

'HOUSE GET SMALLER!' Spit ordered. The house shrunk some more.

'It is still too big to carry,' said Maura. 'Make it as small as an orange.'

'HOUSE, GET AS SMALL AS AN ORANGE!' ordered Spit.

The house got as small as an orange.

'That is perfect,' said Sean. He picked it up. 'Now make it invisible.'

'HOUSE, GET INVISIBLE!' ordered Spit. The house became invisible.

'There are trucks and cars driving along the forest road,' said Veggie. 'It is time for us to get out of here.'

'Spit had better come and sit on my shoulders like he does with Granny when they are driving into Dara,' said Maura.

Spit jumped up on Maura's shoulder and draped himself like a scarf around her neck. 'I hope you won't get too warm,' he said.

'I'll be fine,' said Maura.

With Veggie leading the way, the twins set off through the forest, keeping well away from all paths and trails. The ground was rough and uneven. Sean didn't notice a tree root that protruded high up out of the ground. He tripped over it and, as he fell, he dropped the invisible house.

They could hear Granny and the witch cry out in terror.

Maura said, 'It's all right. We will find you. Veggie, can you nose around and discover where the house is now?'

But Veggie's mind was on other things. He said, 'I think we are about to have visitors.'

The twins and Spit looked around. Coming towards them were two forestry workers and a large dog on a lead.

The dog had got the scent of Veggie and was straining to get free.

'What are we going to do?' whispered Maura.

Veggie said, 'I'll slip off towards the main track. That will attract the dog's attention away from here and the house won't get walked on.'

'Are you sure you will be all right?'

asked Maura and Sean together.

'Oh yes, I know my way through these woods very well. Don't hang around waiting for me. If I don't make it back here I'll meet you at the bridge down on the main road.'

With that Veggie slipped away through the trees, pausing only to make sure that the dog saw him.

The dog became more excited but the man holding the lead hadn't seen Veggie and pulled hard at the lead. 'Take it easy, Boyo,' he said.

'I might just slip away too,' said Spit. 'They might wonder why you have a cat with you.'

Before the twins could stop him the cat jumped down and ran off in the opposite direction to Veggie.

'Let's go and meet them,' Sean said. 'That'll keep them away from here. Be careful where you step. We don't want to squash the house.'

'Well and what brings you two children out here all by yourselves?' the man with the dog asked.

'We heard helicopters and planes,' said Sean. 'Do you know what's going on?'

'Not really. We haven't been able to pick up much on our two-way radio,' the second man said. 'All those helicopters flying around are interfering with reception but there was something about alien crows and flying pigs.'

'I think that's someone's idea of a joke, although I don't know when I've seen Boyo so excited,' the first man said.

Boyo, the dog, had now got the scent of Spit and tried to drag the man in that direction.

'Perhaps there's something that we can't see here in the woods,' Maura said.

Sean nodded in agreement. 'Some people say that a dog can sense things that humans can't.'

'I've heard that too,' the second man said. 'Maybe we should just do our job and clear out of here before we get mixed up in something strange.'

The first man was worried. 'Some one reported seeing smoke. Forest fires can be started very easily and soon get out of control. You two weren't fooling about with matches, were you?'

'No, of course we weren't,' replied Maura.

'Well I can smell something burning,' the man said. 'But it smells like turf and not wood.'

The twins realised that the fire in the witch's kitchen must still be smouldering. 'The smell could be fumes from the planes,' the second man said, looking around nervously as if he expected an alien to pounce on him.

'That's very true. I can see no sign of smoke,' said the first man, happy now for any excuse to leave the forest. 'And it could be a bird that's upsetting Boyo, even though that's never happened before.'

'Did you not say something about alien crows?' Sean asked. 'Could it be one of them?'

'That settles it,' said the second man. 'Let's all get out of here. The truck is parked over there.'

'Don't worry about us,' said Maura. 'We can find our own way home.'

'We wouldn't dream of leaving you here with so much strange stuff going on,' said the man with the dog. 'Where do you live?'

'Drop us at the bridge on the main road,' Sean said. 'We can walk home from there.'

Before they followed the two men and Boyo the twins looked back. Spit was sitting on the highest branch of the tallest pine-tree. He waved to them. With a bit of luck Veggie would be at the bridge by now. They would have to rely on him to lead them back through the forest and find the witch's house. They hoped that Spit would guess what they were planning and that he would be able to reassure Granny that everything would be all right.

The Witch's Story

Granny and the witch got a terrible fright when Sean dropped the house. The broken furniture was scattered around like match-sticks as the house rolled over and over before coming to rest between two pine-trees.

Granny sat still for a few seconds. Then when she had got her breath back she asked the witch, 'Are you all right?'

The witch replied very crossly, 'Oh I am absolutely fine - apart from the fact that I am black and blue, thanks to that grandson of yours!'

Granny resolved not to lose her temper and said very calmly, 'Well at least you haven't broken anything.'

'Not broken anything,' spluttered the witch. 'Would you look at my furniture?

Is that not all broken?'

'Furniture can be replaced,' Granny said. 'And, if my memory serves me right, the furniture was broken long before Sean dropped the house. It got broken when you made the house fly by mistake. And, please, don't tell me that it was not a mistake. We both know that it was.'

'If you and the twins and that fox hadn't interfered, everything would have been all right,' snapped the witch.

Before Granny could reply they heard the sound of Boyo barking outside. They listened carefully to the conversation between the forestry workers and the twins.

When the twins went away with the men and the dog, the witch said, 'Now what are we supposed to do?'

'Sit and wait until we are quite sure that it is all safe,' said Granny. 'And while we are waiting you could please explain why you think that Spit belongs to you.'

'I know just by looking at him that he is my lost cat but he won't confess that he is. He's ashamed of me because he thinks than I am not very good at being a witch.'

'But you are an American witch. Spit is an Irish cat. How would an American witch have a cat that's Irish?'

'We have always had cats from Ireland to help us with our magic,' said the witch.

'Who do mean when you say "we"?' asked Granny.

'Why I mean the famous Leamington witches, of course. Don't tell me that you have never heard of the Leamington witches?'

'No, I haven't.' Granny looked blank.

'We're probably the most famous

witches in the world,' explained the witch.

'If you're that famous why aren't you better at doing things?' asked Granny.

'I don't really know,' admitted the witch. She knew that there was no point in lying to Granny Green. 'I thought that if I came to Ireland and found my cat that things might get better. Space, that's Spit's real name, had been living with me only a very short time before he left.'

The witch now looked so sad that Granny felt sorry for her.

'You have no idea what a disgrace it is for a witch when her cat runs away,' the witch continued. 'It is the very worst thing that can happen to a witch. The other Leamington witches tried to be nice about it but I knew that they were whispering about me.

'Things got steadily worse. One day I promised some friends of mine fine weather for a barbecue. But I got the spells mixed up. Instead of the sun shining there was a cloud-burst. And *only* over the place where the barbecue was being held. It was all a complete wash-out.'

'And that was why you decided to leave Leamington and come and look for your cat?' Granny said. 'How did you hear about Spit?'

'I read in the newspapers about your flying display in the Valley of the Crows and wondered if you were a witch. There are witches in Ireland, you know.'

'So I have been told,' replied Granny. 'But I am not one of them. Another thing that you should know is that Spit couldn't fly when I found him on the side of the road. He learned to fly by watching me, just like the pig did. And Spit has been living with me now for almost three years.'

92

'That is about the time that Space, my cat, disappeared,' said the witch.

'You've been looking for Space for three years?' Granny asked in amazement.

'Yes, but not all the time in Ireland. I looked all over America first. Then a witch that I know in Boston said that maybe I should come and look over here. When I read about Spit I was sure that my search was over. That's why I bought the farmhouse in the valley. I thought that, between us, he and I could learn how to do the magic properly. He wouldn't be ashamed of me any more. Then maybe I would be allowed to go back and live in Leamington. Oh dear ... I didn't mean to tell you that the other witches made me leave Leamington.'

'Because of the cloud-burst at the barbecue?'

'That - and one or two other things

that went wrong. Like the children's birthday party. I made the balloons too big. They carried some of the children into the next county,' said the witch.

'I'm surprised that you want to be a witch at all,' said Granny.

'What else can I do?' asked the witch.

'There must be something,' said Granny. 'But, just to prove to you that Spit is not your cat, let me tell that when I found Spit three years ago he was just a tiny kitten. Your cat would have been fully grown by then. But what we really need to worry about right now is how are we going to get out of here and safely back home.'

'Hello,' a voice outside the house said. Then the house shook as though something had hit it.

'That's Spit,' said Granny. 'The clever thing has found the house. He is touching it with his paw.'

'I hope that he won't damage it even more,' said the witch.

'I'll have a word with him,' said Granny. Then she called out, 'Spit, we can hear you. Is it safe for us to come out of the house?'

'Yes, it is,' said Spit. 'Hold on while I make the house visible again.' He closed his eyes and said: 'UNDO THE INVISIBLE HOUSE SPELL.'

The house suddenly appeared at the

foot of the pine-tree. The front door opened. Granny and the witch came out. They were the size of two small dolls.

Spit said, 'The twins are meeting Veggie down by the bridge. If we hurry we can catch up with them and save them having to come back into the forest. That dog with the forestry workers might get loose and chase after them. Then we would all get caught and be in real trouble.'

'We can't leave my house behind,' protested the witch.

'I've thought about that,' said Spit. 'Is the surfboard still in the downstairs room?'

'Yes, it is, 'said the witch.

'Then bring it out and let's see if it's still in one piece.'

The witch carried the surfboard out into the forest. It was in perfect condition.

'Good,' said Spit. 'Now all we have to do is to make the surfboard big enough to carry the three of us and the house.'

Granny didn't like the sound of this, especially when she thought of how the witch's spells could go wrong. 'Will it be safe?' she asked.

'Of course, it will be safe. If there is one thing that I do know for sure it is how to control my surfboard.' The witch clicked her fingers. The surfboard became long enough for the house and Granny and the witch to fit on it.

Spit said, 'I think you're getting better at making spells work. Now you have to make me small.'

The witch said, 'I think that I can remember that spell. I used to make Space small sometimes.' She closed her eyes, thought for a few seconds and said: 'SEE THE IVY ON THE WALL, SEE THIS CAT AND MAKE HIM SMALL ENOUGH TO

FIT ON THE SURFBOARD.'

Spit at once grew small enough to sit on the surf board with the house clasped firmly between his paws.

'Do we not need water for a surfboard to travel on?' asked Granny.

Spit said, 'A surfboard that can fly across the Atlantic will have no problem going through this forest to the bridge on the main road.'

And Spit was right. The witch gave the surfboard a slap and said: 'TO THE BRIDGE ON THE MAIN ROAD.'

The surfboard took off. It whizzed and zoomed and wound its way around the pine-trees until Granny felt as though she was on the biggest, fastest, newest funfair ride in the world. She also felt quite safe. Yet she was quite pleased when, at last, she could see the twins waiting on the bridge.

Veggie came out of the undergrowth

just as the surfboard arrived. 'So we are all safely out of the forest,' he said. 'You lot had better take the surfboard down along the river and then across the fields to the Valley of the Crows. Stay close to the ground and no one will notice you. The twins and I will go back to Tigín on foot.'

'Why can't we go on the surfboard too?' asked Sean.

'Because the forestry workers will have reported seeing you,' said Veggie. 'People will be keeping an eye out for you. If you vanish, a search party will be sent out to find you. We could all end up in trouble again. It's not far to Tigín. I'll show you a short cut that only foxes know.'

Then the twins and Veggie waved as the surfboard set off to follow the river.

Spit Provides the Answers

Though Veggie had called it a short cut it was late in the afternoon when the twins arrived back at Tigín. There was a delicious smell of food coming from the open door. 'That must be the stew that Granny was cooking for us before this adventure began,' said Maura. 'I'll just go and make sure that it isn't burning.'

Veggie sniffed the air happily and said, 'I'm sure we could all do with a hot meal after all that excitement.'

'There's always meat in Granny's stews. Don't forget that you've turned vegetarian,' Sean said.

'He can just eat the vegetables,' Maura said, as she came back out of the house. 'The food is on a very low heat so it is perfectly all right. Now let's go and find

Granny and Spit and the witch.'

'Why don't we fly up the valley and look for them?' asked Sean.

'Better not, in case there are still any planes about, although I'm sure that Granny and Spit and the witch will take great care not to be seen flying back on the surfboard,' said Veggie as he led the way back into the Valley of the Crows.

In spite of Veggie's reassurance the twins felt their hearts beat faster and faster as they ran along the valley road. It was only when they got to the high rocks and looked down into the hollow and saw that the farmhouse was standing where it had always stood that they dared to breathe a sigh of relief.

The trees around it also looked as they had always looked. The crows were back in their nests, making a terrible noise as they talked over and over the day's adventures. When they saw Veggie and the twins they swooped down to greet them.

'What happened after you flew away from the pine forest?' Sean asked.

'Oh, the planes followed us for a while but we kept changing direction, so that the pilots got all mixed up,' said the senior crow. 'Then a flying pig seemed to come from nowhere. The planes and helicopters all flew off after that.'

'And what about Granny and Spit and the witch?' Maura asked anxiously. 'Did they arrive back safely along with the farmhouse?'

'They most certainly did, They are all inside in the farmhouse right now,' said the senior crow as he frowned in the direction of Veggie. 'How long is the fox going to stay in the valley?'

'Forever and ever,' said Veggie, 'so we might as well be friends.'

'We'll think about that,' said the senior crow. Then he and the other birds flew back to their nests.

The door of the farmhouse opened. Granny and Spit ran out. There were great hugs and kisses all round.

'Where's the witch?' asked Veggie.

'In the kitchen, trying to find a spell for putting furniture and crockery back together. Everything is in bits.'

'Can Spit not fix things for her?' asked Veggie. 'He was very good at making the house appear and disappear.'

'I tried, but it didn't work,' said Spit. 'In fact I don't know how I was able to do any of those other things.'

'The witch thinks it's because you were meant to be a witch's cat – even though she knows that you are not her cat,' said Granny.

'Oh, she has finally admitted that Spit is not her cat, has she?' asked Maura.

103

'Yes,' said Granny. 'Now she's going to look for the cat that really is hers.'

There was a terrible crash from inside the house.

'Oh dear, dear,' said Granny. 'The spell must have gone wrong again!'

And so it had. Instead of mending the crockery and the furniture, the spell had made the stairs fall down. Now the witch couldn't get to her bedroom – unless she flew in through the window.

'And I wouldn't advise you to do that. You might be seen,' said Granny. 'You had better sleep in Tigín tonight. We can get a carpenter in the morning.'

'Witches don't send for carpenters,' said the witch crushingly. 'We do our own repairs. If we could only find my cat, Space, everything would work out fine. Where in tarnation can he be?'

'Maybe Spit could help us find him,' said Veggie, turning to the cat. 'Can you remember how you came to be at the side of the road on that morning that Granny found you?'

'I was playing hide and seek with some of my brothers and my uncle, who was back on a visit. I went too far away from home and got lost. I just kept on walking until I could walk no more. That's when Granny found me.'

'You never told me that before now,' said Granny.

'It didn't seem important until now. I have been too happy in Tigín to wonder about where I came from.'

'But this uncle of yours could be my missing cat,' said the witch. 'Both your names begin with same letter.'

'I gave Spit his name,' said Granny. 'You mustn't look for magic meanings where there aren't any.' She spoke to Spit again. 'Can you remember anything about the place where you were living when your uncle came to visit you?'

'It was a big town with a castle,' said Spit. 'I remember my uncle saying that he had got so homesick for that castle that he just had to come back and see it.'

'Do you remember this uncle's name?' asked the witch.

A glassy look came into Spit's eyes. 'No, not really. I was very young you see. But I do remember that he had a strange accent.' Then he brightened up. 'It could have been an American accent, all mixed up with an Irish one. There is another thing too that I remember. He had a very loud laugh. It would shake the moon in the sky.'

'That is my Space without a shadow of a doubt,' said the witch. 'And that is why you are so clever with spells. You come from a family of cats that, for as long as witches can remember, have hidden on boats to cross the Atlantic ocean to keep magic alive in America.'

'And he didn't come back to Ireland because he was ashamed of you. He came back because he was homesick,' Granny said to the witch. 'Every human and every creature that has ever left Ireland gets homesick. Once he got back he must have decided to stay. He might even have been hoping that you would have to come and look for him. Maybe he is hoping that you will decide to live in Ireland.'

'And so I will now that I have bought this lovely little farmhouse. Space and I could be very happy in the Valley of the Crows,' sighed the witch. 'But where is this city with the castle?'

'Sounds to me like Kilkenny. I know the place quite well,' said Veggie. 'And aren't Kilkenny cats famous the world over for their clever ways?'

'And a famous witch lived there

hundreds of years ago,' said Granny. 'Since you know the city, I think that, as soon as it's dark, you should go with the witch on the surfboard to Kilkenny and help her to find Space.'

'While I'm waiting for it to get dark I'll try out a few spells for mending the furniture and the stairs,' said the witch.

'Are you not hungry?' asked Maura. 'There's a lovely stew cooking over in Granny's.'

'I forgot all about the lunch,' said Granny. 'It'll be ruined.'

'No, it's grand' said Maura.

'Well I am a bit peckish,' said the witch. 'You go on ahead. I'll catch up when I've tried out some more spells.'

As Granny and the others walked back towards Tigín they could hear loud crashes coming from the farmhouse.

'She still doesn't seem to be doing very well with her spells,' said Sean. 'I hope things will get better when she finds Space.'

'Whether they do or not, it is going to be very interesting to have a witch and her cat living so close at hand,' said Granny. 'Just don't say a word to anyone in Dara.'

'We won't,' the twins promised.

Lunch was delicious. They were all so hungry that they had three helping each. Veggie got just vegetables and bread and gravy but the gravy tasted so good that he didn't miss the pieces of meat.

The witch turned up in time to get her share and said it was the best food she had in years. Unfortunately she hadn't managed to fix the furniture or the stairs so she and Space, if she found him, would have to stay that night with Granny Green.

The twins thought it was a great pity that they couldn't stay too but there wouldn't be room for them.

'What will we tell Mum and Dad if they ask us who's the new owner of the farmhouse?' asked Maura. 'They're bound to find out it's been sold.'

'Tell them that it now belongs to Janie MacDonald, for that is my name,' said the witch. 'Say, too, that I am here to live quietly but that I will drive into Dara one day soon with Granny Green to meet everyone.'

'I just hope there's room for two cats in the car,' said Maura.

'Two cats and a fox,' added Veggie.

'No way is a fox coming into Dara in my car,' said Granny Green. 'That would really bring crowds of people out here to see what's going on.'

Granny Green need not have worried about people coming near the Valley of the Crows. Instead they were all heading for the pine forest and the mountains where, according to the TV news, alien pigs and flying saucers had been seen by the Air Corps.

That night before they went to bed the twins looked out the landing window. They thought they saw the surfboard with Janie and Veggie on board setting off for Kilkenny.

At first light next day they cycled as fast as they could back to Tigín. There, sitting on the wall with Spit, was a fine black cat, who said, 'You must be the twins.'

'And you must be Space,' said Maura. 'Are you happy your witch found you?'

'I always knew that she would,' said Space. 'She and Granny are inside having breakfast. You'd think they had known each other for years. My nephew and I have been having a great chat too.'

'He's told me all about our family,'

said Spit. 'We'll come and see you tonight and tell you the whole story.'

The twins were delighted to hear this. Then they had to cycle back to the hotel as fast as they could before they were missed and had to explain why they had to go out to Tigín so early in the morning.

As they reached the hotel Sean said, 'I wonder if Granny will ever find out if her great-grandmother was a witch.'

Maura said, 'I was wondering if the flying pig ever found a place to live. Maybe Spit and Space will see her still flying around in the sky. I can hardly wait for them to visit us tonight.'